DISCARDED

*of related interest*

**ABC of Gender Identity**
*Devika Dalal*
ISBN 978 1 78775 808 7
eISBN 978 1 78775 809 4

**Sylvia and Marsha Start a Revolution!**
The Story of the Trans Women of Color
Who Made LGBTQ+ History
*Joy Michael Ellison and Teshika Silver*
ISBN 978 1 78775 530 7
eISBN 978 1 78775 531 4

**The Every Body Book**
The LGBTQ+ Inclusive Guide for Kids about
Sex, Gender, Bodies, and Families
*Rachel E. Simon, LCSW*
ISBN 978 1 78775 173 6
eISBN 978 1 78775 174 3

**Rainbow Village**
A Story to Help Children Celebrate Diversity
*Emmi Smid*
ISBN 978 1 78592 248 0
eISBN 978 1 78450 533 2

**The Big Book of LGBTQ+ Activities**
Teaching Children about Gender Identity, Sexuality,
Relationships and Different Families
*Amie Taylor*
*Illustrated by Liza Stevens*
ISBN 978 1 78775 337 2
eISBN 978 1 78775 338 9

**The Prince and the Frog**
A Story to Help Children Learn about
Same-Sex Relationships
*Olly Pike*
ISBN 978 1 78592 382 1
eISBN 978 1 78450 731 2

# Me & My Dysphoria Monster

An Empowering Story to Help Children
Cope with Gender Dysphoria

## Laura Kate Dale

Illustrated by Ang Hui Qing

Jessica Kingsley Publishers
London and Philadelphia

First published in Great Britain in 2022 by Jessica Kingsley Publishers
An imprint of Hodder & Stoughton Ltd
An Hachette Company

1

A CIP catalogue record for this title is available from the
British Library and the Library of Congress

ISBN 978 1 83997 092 4
eISBN 978 1 83997 093 1

Printed and bound in China by Leo Paper Products Ltd.

Jessica Kingsley Publishers' policy is to use papers that are natural,
renewable and recyclable products and made from wood grown
in sustainable forests. The logging and manufacturing processes
are expected to conform to the environmental regulations
of the country of origin.

Jessica Kingsley Publishers
Carmelite House
50 Victoria Embankment
London EC4Y 0DZ

www.jkp.com

**Hello!**
My name is
**Nisha.**

And this is my
**monster.**

**My monster follows me everywhere...**

When I go to the beach
with my mum...

When I am taking photos
with my cat...

Even when I play hide
and seek with my friends.

My monster used to be small.
But recently my monster has begun to **grOW.**

When someone refers to
me as a boy, my monster
**grows bigger.**

When people call me by
a boy's name, my monster
**grows larger
and larger.**

When I am told I must use the boys' toilets, my monster **doubles in size.**

And when my teacher tells me I must play on the boys' team, my monster grows **bigger than a giant..**

I don't like being called a boy.
Something just doesn't feel right.

**And I really don't like my monster.**

But my monster doesn't listen.

**My monster only listens to everyone else.**

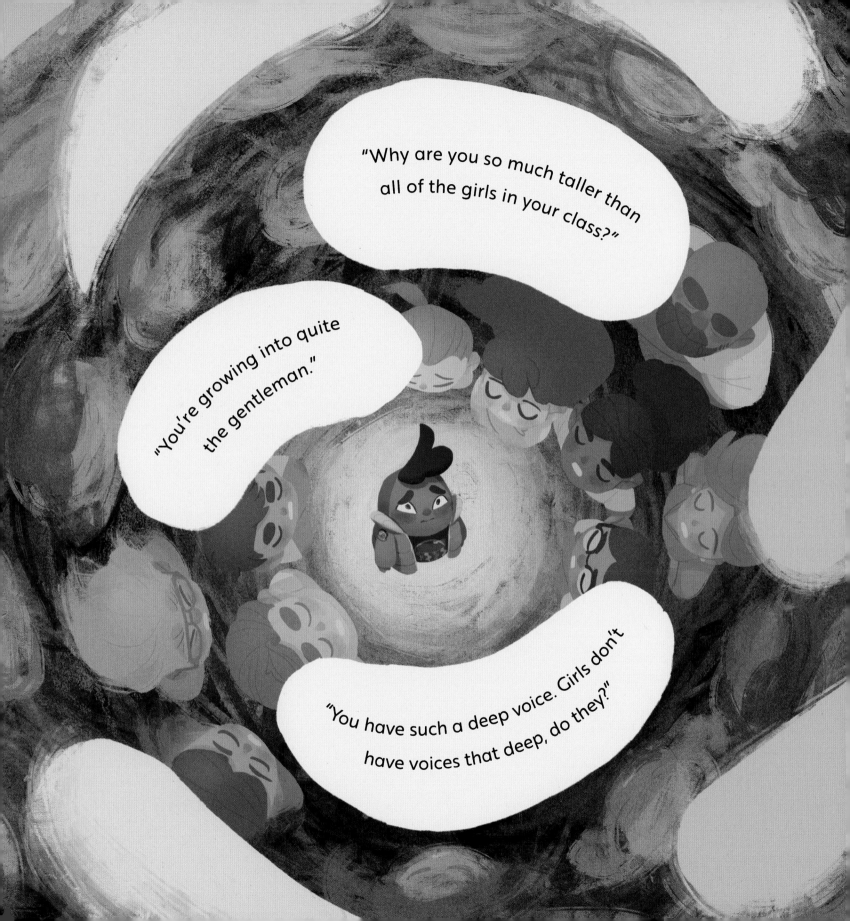

And my monster grows and **grows and grows...**

Until my monster is so huge
it starts getting in my way.

When I go to the
beach with my mum,
my monster doesn't
let me swim.

When my friends invite
me to play, my monster
doesn't let me join.

I feel very alone. I no longer feel like myself any more.

And nobody seems able to scare my monster away.

One day my dad introduced me
to one of his friends.

His name is
**Jack**
and he has a
**monster just
like mine.**

"But sometimes the doctor isn't right. Sometimes people are told they are a **boy**, when actually that person knows they are a **girl**."

"Or sometimes people are told they are a **girl**, when they know they are a **boy**. And for some people, they will grow up and not feel like a boy or a girl at all, but people will continue to call them a boy or a girl."

"When that happens, people like you and me will get a visit from our **gender dysphoria monster**. Our monster is that little voice that knows who we are and who we want to be when we grow up, and it doesn't like to be ignored!"

"First, I told some adults about how I felt. I told them **I was a boy**, and **not a girl**, and I wanted to use a new name and the pronouns **he/him/his**."

"They let me use the name I liked and let me change my clothes and hair, and most importantly, they made sure everyone knew that I was a boy."

"The monster still visits sometimes, but very rarely, and it's very small and quiet when it does."

After speaking with Jack, **I was very happy.**

I talked with my parents, and they stopped using my boy's name and called me Nisha. They used she/her/hers pronouns when talking about me.

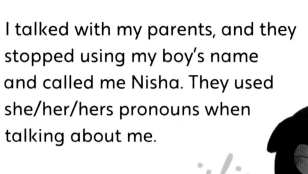

And they let me wear the clothes I felt most comfortable in.

I was still the same person I had always
been, I just changed some things so that
**I was happier about myself.**

And with every little change, my monster began to **Shrink**.

When someone called me a girl, I smiled and my monster grew smaller.

When I used the girls' toilets at school, my monster became **smaller and smaller.**

And when they let me play on the girls' team,
my monster shrank to the size of a

pea.

While my monster still visits me sometimes,
I don't mind seeing it every now and again,
as I know what it's trying to tell me.

I began to swim in the sea again.

I said

**"YES!"**

to my friends when they asked me to play.

I started to become a **happier,** more confident **person.**

And in time, I grew up to become the
**happy, smiling woman**
# I always wanted to be.

The End

# ADULTS' GUIDE

## Useful Terminology and Explanations

This guide aims to offer adults useful terminology, which they may find helpful as a supplement to this book. Terms included may not be directly involved in this story but offer a vocabulary for answering questions children might have about gender.

While people typically use sex and gender interchangeably, because for most people these two line up, when talking with or about trans and non-binary people, you may find them used as two separate concepts.

**Sex** A person's sex typically is used to refer to physical aspects of a person relating to their body. Does their body produce testosterone or oestrogen? Do they have a vagina or a penis? Usually, this is recorded at birth, and is based on physical observations of a baby. In the absence of other factors, a doctor will look at a baby with a penis and register their sex as male on a birth certificate, or register their sex as female if the baby has a vagina.

Depending on your country, sex is not an unchangeable fact on legal paperwork. For example, in the UK, a trans person who has been granted a Gender Recognition Certificate by the government can get a new birth certificate, where their sex is listed to match their gender rather than the observations made at birth.

In the United States, a person can change the sex on their birth certificate in most states. Currently, Tennessee is the only state that has no pathway for changing birth certificate sex, though some states do require either proof of undergoing transition-related surgery, or court hearings with a judge. The United States doesn't have a single process for legally changing sex as recorded on a birth certificate, but most states have pathways to achieve that.

**Gender** Typically used to refer to a person's inherent internal sense of self. When someone talks about their gender identity, they might, for example, mean that while they have a beard and penis, they feel deeply that they are female despite these physical factors.

**Gender Assigned at Birth** Exactly what it sounds like. At birth, a doctor will observe a child's body and decide what sex to register on their birth certificate, assuming that their gender matches that.

**Intersex** Intersex is an umbrella term used to discuss people whose sex doesn't fit neatly into male or female. Around 1% of people worldwide fit under this umbrella, which can cover anything from a person having a chromosomal difference that never physically manifests, to a person having physical development that is a mix of what might be expected from male or female development. Intersex children are usually registered as male or female on birth certificates, and may in some cases have surgery performed as infants to make them fit more neatly into a binary gender box. Intersex people are fighting to stop these surgeries, as they are performed before the person is old enough to consent to the choice of how their body should be altered.

While this book isn't directly about the experiences of intersex people, it is important to note that some intersex people do identify as transgender and/or non-binary, often if their gender identity doesn't align with surgical choices doctors made when they were young. The existence of intersex people shouldn't be used to win arguments about transgender people's validity, but they do exist, and sometimes are trans. For instance, if an intersex person is listed as female on their birth certificate but grows up with a gender identity that is male, they may identify as trans.

**Social Transition** In this book, when Nisha got new clothes and changed her name to feel more comfortable, these were examples of social transition. Social transition is about living as a new gender in social roles, outside of the medical system.

Using myself as an example, I started my transition by socially transitioning. I asked my family and friends to call me Laura and use female pronouns, I started to dress differently, and I started to identify myself as female when asked by others. I hadn't taken any medications or had any surgery, but I was living socially as a woman. I had socially transitioned. When we talk about children transitioning, we are always talking exclusively about social transition. When a trans child picks a new name, tries new pronouns and clothes, they can see whether this alleviates their dysphoria and helps them to feel better before making a decision to physically transition when they are older.

**Medical Transition** Medical transition is all of the parts of transition a doctor is involved in, which require waiting lists and assessments. As an adult, a trans person might go to a doctor to get medication that puts their current puberty on hold. They may start Hormone Replacement Therapy to develop physical characteristics that align more with their gender, and may eventually get surgery to alter aspects of their body. Transition-related surgeries are never performed on children and typically require several years of doctors' visits before anything moves forward.

Any medication offered in late teens, such as hormone delaying medication, is reversible, and can be halted if the teen changes their mind about how they feel.

**Binary** In discussions of transgender experiences, binary as a term is used to talk about people who identify as a gender that is the binary opposite of their gender assigned at birth, so someone assigned male at birth who tells you they are female, or vice versa.

**Non-Binary** This is an umbrella term for identities that don't neatly fit the binary box. A non-binary person might feel like their gender sits somewhere in between male and female, or somewhere outside of the binary line between those two points. They might lean a little either way of centre, but not feel comfortable fully on either side of the spectrum. They may feel they sit directly at the centre point. They may feel like their gender identity doesn't feel like it has a place in that binary discussion at all. Basically, any experience that's in the space between, or outside of, the binaries.

**Gender Non-Conforming** In our current society, there are a lot of actions, behaviours, activities and styles of clothing that are typically considered to be gendered in some way. For instance, parents try trucks for boys and dolls for girls, skirts for girls and bow ties for boys, etc. A girl may really like playing with trucks, and a boy might be really into ballet, but that doesn't mean they are always transgender. They may simply be gender non-conforming.

There is a difference between a person's inherent internal sense of their gender, and the way they engage with things that are seen as gendered in the world. A person could be perfectly comfortable being a woman, but really enjoy doing activities that society says are masculine, like repairing classic car engines. Gender is a spectrum, and the gendering of many things are social constructs.

So no, just because your kid picks up and plays with a toy that's not designed with their gender in mind, that doesn't mean they're trans, or that doctors are going to push them to transition. To feel inherently like your gender differs is a very separate and distinct experience.

**Agender** Some people live with a feeling of not having a gender at all. It's not that they feel somewhere in the middle of the spectrum, rather they might feel off to one side, away from the whole discussion.

**Gender Fluid** Some people's experience of gender shifts over time. Someone might feel male at one point in time, but at others feel female. Gender identity isn't always a fixed, immutable thing.

**Gender Dysphoria** The feeling of distress and disconnect experienced by many transgender people when they are forced to experience their gender assigned at birth. From being referred to by the wrong pronouns, to feeling excluded from gendered friendships or activities, to feeling upset about changes to appearance that have traditionally gendered connotations, it's basically a looming feeling of wrongness.

**Gender Euphoria** The inverse of gender dysphoria, a positive and affirming feeling that comes as a result of having your gender identity recognized by others, or engaging in gender-affirming activities.

**Cisgender** The term Cis, or Cisgender, functions as an antonym for transgender. Much as we use the term "straight" to describe people who are not in any way same sex or same gender attracted, we use cisgender to describe people whose gender identity lines up with their sex assigned at birth.

## QUESTIONS

**Are Gender Identity and Sexuality connected?** No, not at all. For example, a trans woman can be gay, straight, bisexual, or any other sexuality, just like a cis woman can. Gender identity is who you feel you are, and sexuality is who you are attracted to. You could be attracted to men and feel like a woman, or be attracted to men and feel like a man. The two are not inherently interlinked.

**What is Deadnaming?** When a trans person refers to their deadname, they are usually referring to their old name, prior to transition. The act of deadnaming is when someone, knowing a trans person has come out and changed their name, still uses their old name, either through a lack of care and attention, or as a deliberate malicious act.

It is important, when talking about trans people, not to deadname them when talking about them in the past tense, or prior to their transition. For example, in this story we use the name Nisha throughout, and never tell you the character's previous name, as a matter of respect. The same is true when a celebrity such as Elliot Page comes out as trans. The trans person may not have always had the words to tell you who they are, or been ready to share that information, but that is always who they have been, and the respectful thing to do is avoid using their deadname where possible.

**What does the term misgendering mean?** Similar to deadnaming, misgendering is the deliberate or careless use of gendered terms or pronouns that do not match those a trans person now uses. If a trans woman goes by exclusively she/her pronouns, to refer to her using terms like he, him or sir would be misgendering.

In this story, we would always refer to Nisha using she/her pronouns, even before she has come out. Similar to deadnaming, it's respectful to use a trans person's current pronouns, even when referring to them in the past tense, or prior to their transition.

**What support might a doctor in this story have provided, and at which ages?** In the UK, most transgender care options for children and teens are non-medical interventions. A trans child or teen might change their name, clothes, hairstyle and pronouns, and in some cases may speak to a therapist or mental health professional about their feelings.

**What should you do if a child shares with you that they think they might be trans?** According to the American Psychological Association, as well as the testimonies from transgender people themselves, the right way to respond to a child coming to you and telling you that they are trans, or trying to explain that subject to you with different language (e.g. "I feel like I am meant to be a boy"), is to embrace affirmative care.

Nobody is a better judge of someone's gender than the person themselves, and that includes children. While some people may joke about "my kid pretended to be a dog all day, should I believe they're a dog?" and similar statements, at the core there is a difference between light-hearted make-believe and inherent sense of self.

If a child is coming to you, seeming distressed and/or sincere, and tells you they want to be a different gender from the one you have been treating them as, the best advice is to support that. Ask if they want to change anything, such as clothes, name or hair. Allow them the room to try social transition and see if it sticks.

If they later decide they want to change back to how they were before, nothing has ultimately been harmed, life goes on. But, for a child whose feelings of being trans persist, that early support and affirmation will make a huge difference to their confidence and mental health.

Affirming care from the start allows your child to explore who they are safely, and to know that it's okay for them to be who they want to be without needing to hide that.

**Where can you find help and support if a child you know comes out as transgender?** In the UK, charities such as Mermaids offer great support and resources for adults who want to learn how to support trans children in their lives. In the US, Human Rights Campaign have a variety of useful information on their website.

While the places to seek support differ by country, you should be looking for groups that expressly support the affirmative care model. Steer clear of any resources that suggest trans status is a social fad or that it can be cured through therapy.